W9-CAY-497

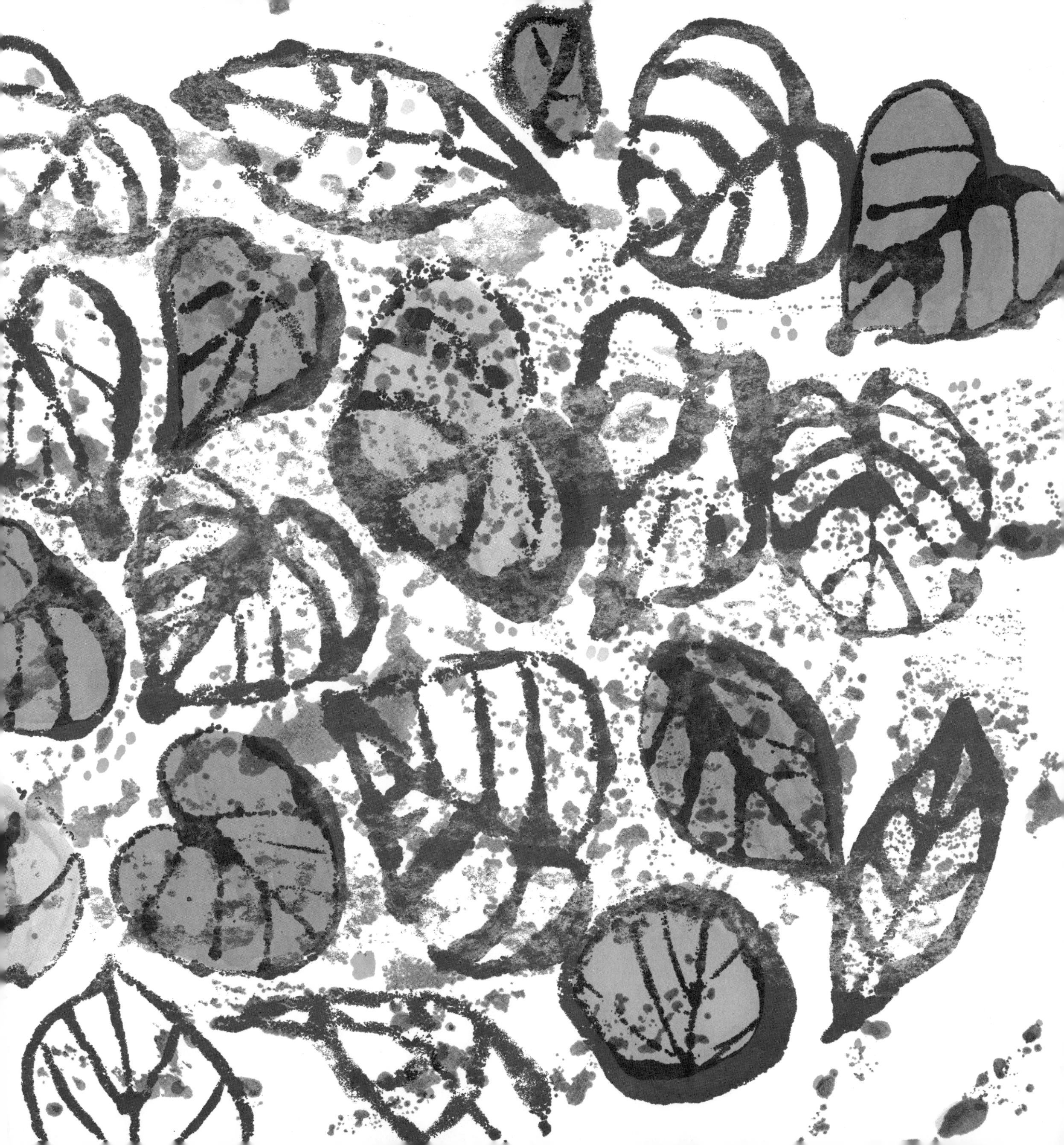

You Look Ridiculous

Said the Rhinoceros to the Hippopotamus

by Bernard Waber

HOUGHTON MIFFLIN CO.
BOSTON

for Anne

Printed in the United States of America

WOZ 20 19 18 17 16 15

Once upon a time in the jungle . . .

a rhinoceros came upon a hippopotamus
splashing about in the mud.
"You look ridiculous," said the rhinoceros
to the hippopotamus.

"But I like mud," answered the hippopotamus.
"Oh, it isn't the mud that makes you look ridiculous," said the rhinoceros. "It's your nose."
The hippopotamus looked down at her nose.
"What's wrong with my nose?" she asked.

"You don't see anything missing?" the rhinoceros asked.
The hippopotamus shook her head.
"You don't see a horn missing?" the rhinoceros asked again.
"A horn?" said the hippopotamus.
"A horn," said the rhinoceros.
"Your nose doesn't have a horn and a nose without
a horn looks absolutely ridiculous."
Raising herself from the mud, the hippopotamus
looked down at her nose once more. When she looked
up again, the rhinoceros was gone.

If only I had a horn, like the rhinoceros, I wouldn't
look ridiculous, thought the hippopotamus.
That's the way it was with the hippopotamus.
Once a worrisome thought was put into her head, she would
fret and fuss and fume and just never let go of it.
There was only one way to settle it, she decided.
She would go and ask everyone she met if they too
thought she looked ridiculous.

First she met a lion.
"Do you think I look ridiculous?"
she asked the lion.
The lion thought about it.
"Well, if it's an honest opinion you want . . ."
the lion began at last.
"Yes," said the hippopotamus.
"Then I must say you do look ridiculous.
Look at you," said the lion, "you haven't
got a mane. What you need is a glorious mane
like mine."
The lion shook his mane just to prove how
truly glorious it was.
"No hard feelings, I hope," said the lion.
"No hard feelings," answered the hippopotamus sadly.

If only I had a glorious mane,
like the lion,
I wouldn't look ridiculous,
thought the hippopotamus
continuing her walk.

She met a leopard.
"Do you think I look ridiculous?"
she asked the leopard.
The leopard studied the hippopotamus carefully.
"Now that you mention it . . ." the leopard began.
"Yes," said the hippopotamus.
"I would say you do look ridiculous. Look at you,"
said the leopard, "you have no spots.
What you need is a handsomely spotted
coat like mine."
The leopard gave a good, long stretch to show
off every last spot on his handsome coat.
"We're still friends, I hope," said the leopard.
"We're still friends," answered the hippopotamus sadly.

If only I had handsome spots, like the leopard,
I wouldn't look ridiculous,
thought the hippopotamus continuing her walk.

She met an elephant.
"Do you think I look ridiculous?"
she asked the elephant.
The elephant seemed surprised by the question.
"I have to think about it," he said.
The hippopotamus waited while the
elephant thought.
"Aha," said the elephant,
"I know what it is."
"What?" asked the hippopotamus eagerly.
"You have no ears."
"No ears?" said the hippopotamus.
"No ears to speak of," said the elephant.
"What you need are big, floppy ears
like mine."
The elephant flopped his ears to prove his point.
"See what I mean?" said the elephant.
"I see," answered the hippopotamus sadly.

If only I had big, floppy ears, like the elephant,
I wouldn't look ridiculous,
thought the hippopotamus continuing her walk.

She met a monkey.
"Do you think I look ridiculous?" she asked the monkey.
"If you call not having a tail ridiculous, then I
would say you look ridiculous," answered the monkey.
"No tail?" said the hippopotamus.
"No tail to speak of," said the monkey.
"Look at me," continued the monkey,
"I am not nearly your size and I have
a magnificent tail."
With that, the monkey scrambled up a tree and
swung from a branch by his tail.
"Nothing personal of course," the monkey
called down.
"Of course not," the hippopotamus answered sadly.

If only I had a magnificent tail,
like the monkey,
I wouldn't look ridiculous,
thought the hippopotamus
continuing her walk.

She met a giraffe.
"Do you think I look ridiculous?" she asked the giraffe.
"Of course you look ridiculous," said the giraffe
getting to the point at once.
"You have no neck."
"No neck?" said the hippopotamus.
"No neck to speak of," said the giraffe.
"How can you possibly see the world
without a neck?"
"I see flowers, I see birds, I see the stars
at night . . ." began the hippopotamus.
"Ah, but do you see the treetops?
Do you see the distant hills?
Of course not," said the giraffe
answering her own questions.
"What you need is a long, long neck like mine."
With that the giraffe stretched out her neck until
it seemed her head would disappear into the clouds
and she went about the business of seeing the world.
"I think you're very nice otherwise," the giraffe
called back over her shoulder.
"Thank you," answered the hippopotamus sadly.

If only I had a long, long neck,
like the giraffe,
I wouldn't look ridiculous,
thought the hippopotamus
continuing her walk.

She met a turtle.
"Do you think I look ridiculous?" she asked the turtle.
"I suppose someone should tell you," said the turtle.
"Yes," said the hippopotamus.
"You do look ridiculous without a shell."
"A shell?" said the hippopotamus.
"Oh, they're wonderful," said the turtle. "I couldn't live without one. My shell is my house. It keeps me warm when it is cold and cool when it is hot. And if I ever need a place to hide," said the turtle, backing into her shell, "I know exactly where to go. You'd have found out sooner or later," the turtle called out from inside her little house.
"I suppose," answered the hippopotamus sadly.

If only I had a wonderful shell, like the turtle,
I wouldn't look ridiculous,
thought the hippopotamus continuing her walk.

She met a nightingale.
"Do you think I look ridiculous?" she asked the nightingale.
"If you don't mind my saying so, I think you
sound ridiculous," said the nightingale.
"What you need is a beautiful voice
like mine. Listen," said the nightingale.
And the nightingale sang a beautiful but sad
song for the hippopotamus.
Suddenly the hippopotamus could not bear
to continue her walk or ask further questions.
"I am a ridiculous creature," she sighed.
"I shall find a place to hide and never
show myself to anyone again."

The hippopotamus ran and ran until she found
a lonely place where no one would find her.
"Why did I have to be born looking so ridiculous?"
she cried as she fell asleep that night.
While sleeping she began to dream.
And as so often happens in dreams, her dearest
of wishes were granted.

She dreamed she had a horn
like the rhinoceros's, a mane like the lion's, spots
like the leopard's, ears like the elephant's, a tail like
the monkey's, a neck like the giraffe's, a shell like the turtle's
and a voice like the nightingale's.
So delighted was the hippopotamus with her new appearance
she ran to show herself off to everyone.
"Look at me," she called out in
her sweet nightingale voice,
"I no longer look ridiculous."

Everyone laughed when they saw the new hippopotamus.
The monkey laughed so hard he almost fell
out of his tree.
"What is wrong?" cried the hippopotamus.
"Why do you laugh? Can't you see for
yourselves I no longer look ridiculous?"
This only made the animals laugh even more.

The hippopotamus rushed to a rain puddle to see
for herself.
"Ohhh . . ." she cried out upon seeing her reflection,
"I LOOK RIDICULOUS."
She was so shaken by what she saw,
she shook herself awake.

"Thank goodness it was only a dream,"
the hippopotamus sighed with relief.
Joyfully she plopped herself into the nearest
mudhole and from that day to this,
is proud to be just what she is—

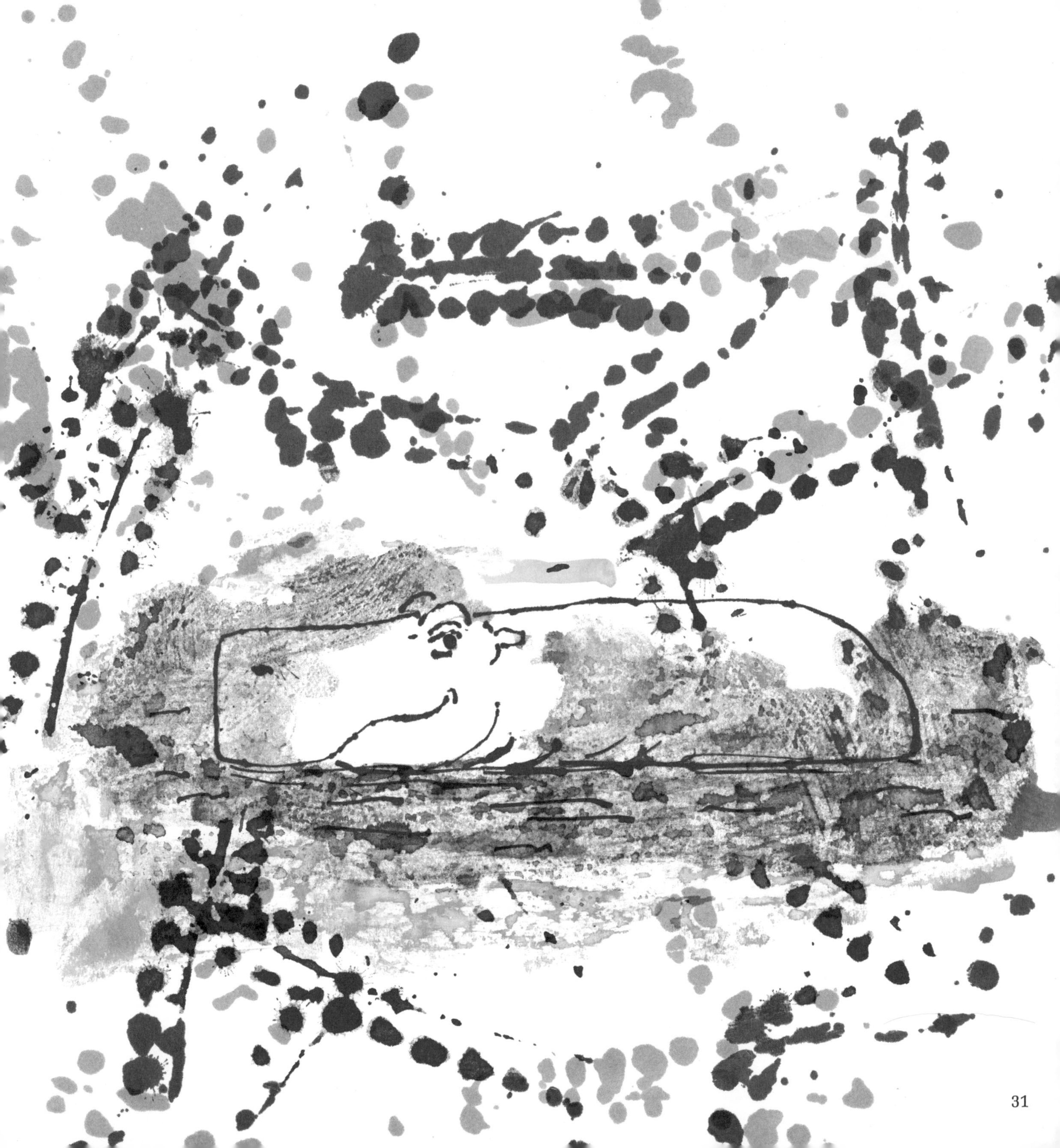

a big, fat, wonderful hippopotamus.